ETHEREAL REALMS

CHRONICLES OF CLAMP

Tanish Nandanwar

PRACHI
DIGITAL PUBLICATION

ISBN : 9789348332967
Edition : First, August 2025
Title : Ethereal Realms- Chronicles of Clamp
Author : Tanish Nandanwar

Published by

PRACHI
DIGITAL PUBLICATION

Regd. Add.: 254, Khuriyakhatta No. 10, Bindukhatta,
Lalkuan, Nainital - 262402, Uttarakhand, India
Website : www.prachidigital.com
E-mail : info@prachidigital.in
Phone : +91 976041 7980, +91 976041 8103

Printed by :
Manipal Technologies Limited, Bengaluru - 560001, Karnataka

INDEX

Acknowledgement

This story has been a collaborative endeavor enriched by the talents and dedication of remarkable individuals who have become cherished partners in the creative process. To Nikhil Yadav, whose artistic prowess brought the characters and landscapes to life with vivid imagery, I extend my deepest gratitude.

To my family, friends, and critique partners and teachers, thank you for your unwavering support and invaluable feedback. To the readers who join this journey, your engagement brings the story to life in ways I could never imagine.

This story is a testament to the power of collaboration and community, and I am immensely grateful for each individual who contributed to its creation. With heartfelt thanks.

Tanish Nandanwar

The Beginning

Once, in a distant galaxy far away from Earth, there existed a mystical realm known as Mesophia. There were all types of herbs, medicine present in this land everyone lived in peace but nobody knew what was going to strike them they were unaware what great war there would be in the future waiting for them. In this ethereal realm, peculiar creatures known as Wheezers resided. One Wheezer known as Clamp, was unlike any other. With his shimmering iridescent scales and wise, amber eyes, he possessed an unparalleled courage and strength and an insatiable desire for peace and harmony throughout the cosmos. Clamp was born with a unique set of skills and abilities. He was chosen by the ancient spirits to protect the realm from any harm that was yet to come. His ultimate goal was to maintain peace and harmony throughout the universe.

Unaware of all these possibilities!

As the sun dipped below the horizon, painting the sky in hues of gold and crimson, Clamp embarks on a journey to spread his message of tranquility to the farthest corners of the universe. Join us on the wonderful series of journey of Clamp in which he finds new friends, allies and even monsters.

1. The Strange Dream

As Clamp soared through the City, he encountered a cloud named Nimbus," Clamp greeted Nimbus warmly, his voice soft and melodious. "What infinite wonders have you witnessed today? "The cloud rumbled softly, shifting and changing shape as it responded, "Clamp, my friend, I have witnessed the dance of comets and the birth of new stars. But I have also witnessed battles and destruction inflicted upon innocent worlds". "Let's meet at the Dragon Ford Field tomorrow at 23 in the evening sharp".

Said Clamp "Very well" Said Nimbus "Bye". Both returned to their home and had a good night sleep meanwhile in Clamp's house when he was sleeping—

"Please! Please, don't hurt me—don't destroy Mesophia! I'm begging you!" Clamp screamed, his body writhing beneath the sheets. Sweat poured down his face as he trembled in his sleep, gripped by a nightmare so vivid it tore the words from his throat like a wounded animal. His voice cracked with terror, each plea laced with heartbreak and panic.

"Mwahahaha You or your Mesophia can't even save yourself, I am going to destroy you and your whole Mesophia in minutes and take all the cliff chives herb to make myself immortal" Said someone in a very heavy voice. Nooooo! Clamp woke up to find that it was all a dream but then he wondered "This dream is coming to me from a while now is there a reason behind this should I tell my Friend Nimbus about this, I think I should but who is the man who always come to destroy

Mesophia... in my dreams?" Clamp muttered to himself, puzzled. Shaking off the lingering haze of sleep, he geared up, grabbed his Yako Mahi fruit—a rare fruit that granted him Super Jump abilities—and launched into the sky in his sleek jet-mobile. With his Space-o-Meter boosting speed, he soared toward Dragon Ford Field, arriving precisely at time.

"Greetings, Nimbus," Clamp said, his tone shifting slightly. "Let's head up to Dew Mountain. There's something I need to talk to you about." "Very well, let's go," Nimbus nodded. Together, they climbed the misty slopes of Dew Mountain. When they reached a quiet ridge, Clamp turned to his friend, concern etched on his face.

"Nimbus... I've been having the same strange dream for the past four or five nights. In it, someone wearing a black mask appears. He says he's going to destroy all of Mesophia and steal the Cliff Chieves to make himself immortal."

Nimbus frowned. "I'm sorry, I don't

know anything about that... but I do know someone who might be able to help us."

"Who?" Clamp asked, eyes narrowing.

"The old queen of Mesophia—Queen Alinbell. She was the last ruler before the Protectors took over. She now lives near the Protection Tree and the Frozen Lake. If anyone understands what's happening to you, it's her," Nimbus said confidently.

"Wait—doesn't she get cold living near a frozen lake?" Clamp asked.

Nimbus chuckled. "Nope. She's an Ice and Water Element user. She's used to it. By the way... did you know everyone in Mesophia has two elemental affinities? But there's a rumour, a prophecy, that one person will awaken a third element. And that person... will become the Superior Protector."

Very well farewell I have to go now, we will go to Alinbell's house tomorrow morning and don't forget to bring your space-o-meter, devangel fruit- a mythical fruit that grants the ability to dodge every attack for one whole day, and your Space-jet" said Nimbus "Very well, see you tomorrow" replied Clamp and they both went their homes. Clamp went to his house had his Mushroom and cheese pizza for dinner and slept tight because he knew he had a big day up in front of him.

2. The Superior Protector's Rumor

The day passed and the next day came, Clamp got ready, took all his things, had his breakfast and left his house eagerly to go to Nimbus's place. Nimbus and Clamp talked a bit and then left with the Space Jet to Alinbell's house. They came across many different and beautiful places. Nimbus said to Clamp that "Do you know friend, that Alinbell can sometimes be mad if anyone doesn't respect her so we have to make sure that we pay her good respect." But they didn't know what was going to come on them Soon there came a rumbling noise from the Jet, it was about to crash down!. Clamp and Nimbus were panicking but suddenly a mysterious figure appeared and saved both from the crash but as soon as it saved both Clamp and Nimbus it disappeared. "Glad we are saved Clamp" said Nimbus Panting "Yes but who was that who saved us?" replied Clamp curiously. "Oh let's not think about that much, the most important to us is now that how will we get to Alinbell's house now?" asked Nimbus "Ohhh don't worry about it I have the Mech-ox -a tool that can fix anything in 1 hour. But the problem is that it is Mech-ox Jr. which will be able to fix the

Jet in 3 hours" replied Clamp. "Very well I guess So ." Said Nimbus. A few hours later the jet-mobile was finally mended "let's go the Jet is finally mended now we can go to Alinbell's house" said Clamp cheerfully. "yes now we can finally go" replied Nimbus.

So they continued their journey to Alinbell's house Soon they Reached Alinbell's house "frrrrrrr it's freezing out here do you think that we can go home I just want to eat my favorite mustard potato strips with my berry seasoning and ketchup." Said Clamp. "So do you think that the frozen lake will be warm? of course it is cold, it is the frozen lake" replied Nimbus as he was little bad-tempered. "We have reached the house" said Nimbus. They reached the house but to their surprise it was empty and no one was inside "You sure that this is the house because I see no one inside" Said Clamp "I am 100% sure that this is the house and see there is also a letter inside." Replied Nimbus "Let's see it," said Clamp. The letter was of Alinbell which said that

LETTER

Hello, Alinbell here and this is a serious message to the superior protector of Mesophia. I am here to inform that I have been captured by the evil sorcerer. The Sorcerer will capture all the protectors of Mesophia one by one and then he will take all the herbs and use them to destroy Mesophia. Only the superior protector can stop him from destroying Mesophia who will have 3 elements and will be a wheezer who wants peace and harmony over the world. Saving the entire cosmos is now upto the protector's hands.

ALINBELL

"Our Mesophia is hopeless" Said Nimbus dreadfully "No, stop thinking like that I think that we won't be able to stop that evil sorcerer alone, I think that we need some new members for our squad" replied Clamp bravely

"Do you really think that we will be enough to stop that evil sorcerer?" Said Nimbus "I don't know but we can still try, otherwise what else can we do to protect our Mesophia." Replied Clamp. "Uhh I am not sure but ok let's go and find some new members for our crew." Said Nimbus, "by the way did you see that it was written a wheezer would be the superior protector of Mesophia I think that protector is you who will have the 3 elemental powers but still everyone gets their elemental powers by the Santana test so we are not pretty much sure that the superior protector will be you," said Nimbus. "I don't know Nimbus but now I am very much tired so I want to go home" Replied Clamp.

After this Both of the two friends returned to Mesophia and went their own ways. Clamp went to his house had his dinner and went to sleep wondering about the rumour of the wheezer which was in the letter but he didn't know that a big day was about to come into his life.

3. The Santana Test

The day has finally come it was the day of Santana Test, the test from which one's element is decided. Every year this test is conducted for the students of Mesophia this test was compulsory about for all of the people that live in Mesophia. This test was very important for Nimbus and Clamp because they wanted to find out that what was the destiny of Clamp whether he would be the protector or not. This time the test was held in the Fiery Fountain. In which, Mr. Magma was taking the test. "Do you think that we will be able to find out about you?" Asked Nimbus Curiously "This is the only way we can find it" answered Clamp. "If it is true then you will be the superior protector of Mesophia, just imagine how much veneration you will get and those tasty pine roots as a gift when you rescue Mesophia from that evil monster" said Nimbus excitedly "yes but I am a little bit worried because if that evil monster has captured Alinbell then how powerful he would be" replied Clamp. "Don't worry friend, we will surely defeat that evil monster no matter how powerful he is" said Nimbus.

Just then Mr. Molten Magma enters into the examination hall

"As you all know today is the

Santana Test, let me remind you all the instructions of the test this test will be of 2 categories- Examination and Practical. First is the examination category so everyone take their test paper and solve them." Said Mr. Magma "Goodness these questions are tough- what is the history of Mesophia." Said Clamp "Not for me because I studied these chapters." Replied Nimbus.

Few hours later the test was finished and it was the time for lunch.

"The time is about to come next is the Practical test which will determine your element Clamp!" Said Nimbus.

The time has finally come everyone went to their separate halls for the practical

"It is finally time let's do the practical" said Clamp to himself. "Let's see this goes here that goes there yes I finally got it" Clamp went on.

The practical was over and everyone was in the main hall for their results to be announced.

"Greetings Clamp how did it go?" asked Nimbus "It was really nice, how was yours" replied Clamp "It was very nice for me too" "Attention please everyone, this is the results for the examination paper, so the first prize goes to Nimbus Cloakez who scored 98%! Congratulations Nimbus for this achievement. Now for the second prize there are not one, not two, but three students who are Clamp Wheezer,

Storia Nestulo and Robes Polesi who scored 92% each. And now for the third prize there is Polinia Stoinis who scored 90% congratulations to all. Now let's see the results and elements of the practical test So the first prize goes to Clamp Wheezer who got straight A++ on all of his practical and as a result he has got- wait what why are there three elements written on this Fire, Thunder and Light" Mr. Molten said "I think he is the superior protector of Mesophia" others mumbled. "You were correct, you are the superior protector of Mesophia I think we should go now because the results are already told, let's go to my favorite Restaurant we will eat something in the celebration of

you becoming the Superior protector of Mesophia" said Nimbus "Yes let's go but I still don't believe that" Replied Clamp. So, they went to 100 elester restaurant that was nearby "Let's eat the Fried Ramen with a soft cheese latte and some butter Rice." Said Clamp. "Very well" replied Nimbus So they ate their food and went to their houses to sleep they both were very excited that they will now be able to beat the evil sorcerer but they still had a lot to know about the evil sorcerer.

4. The Evil Sorcerer

Meanwhile, in the heart of the obsidian fortress—shrouded in shadow and perched high on the jagged cliffs of Dreadspire—a cold, echoing voice rang through the halls.

"Well, well... Bot-20," hissed the evil sorcerer, his voice harsh like grinding steel. "What whispers from Mesophia have you brought me today?"

Bot-20 bowed mechanically, eyes glowing faintly. "Actually, my lord, there is nothing extraordinary—except... the people are speaking of the old Wheezer again."

Drake's crimson eyes narrowed. "Wheezer?"

"Yes, sir. Clamp. That's the name. The one they're calling the 'Superior Protector of Mesophia.' Rumors say he bears not one, but three elements."

A crackle of energy shimmered around Drake. "Hah! So they think that wrinkled fool can protect their precious Mesophia?" he snarled. "No one can stop me now. Not when I wield the three darkest elements in existence: Dark, Water, and Shadow!"

At that moment, a smoother voice broke the tension. "My Lord Drake, your lunch is ready."

Another robot wheeled in a silver tray of delicacies—all meticulously arranged, each dish crowned with a blood-red fruit known as Scarlet Thorneberry. The aroma of strange spices filled the air.

"How is it, Your Majesty?" asked Bot-20 with curiosity.

Drake took a bite, then scowled slightly. "Too much Lestuana—salt and pepper," he muttered. Then, almost fondly, "But still, better than the garbage I ate in my childhood..."

Bot-20 leaned closer. "We will rule over the cosmos soon, right? But... we still need to get rid of that Wheezer."

Drake's gaze turned distant. "Yes... I saw him. He's brave. Clever. But it won't matter... because they do not know the pain I carry. They don't know how I got these powers."

Bot-20 tilted his head. "How did you get three elements, my lord?"

Drake's voice dropped to a growl, bitter and broken. "You want to know? Then listen carefully."

"Once, I was like them—a hopeful child from the storm-washed village of Virellin. I studied at the Felisoca Academy, dreaming to become a Protector of Mesophia. But the others... they only saw the way I looked. My pale eyes, my hunched posture, the way I spoke. They mocked me. They called me 'the Cursed Child.'

I tried to ignore them. I trained hard. But it never mattered. One day, they locked me in the Ice Chamber overnight as a prank. I nearly froze. When I finally escaped, something inside me shattered.

That night, I found a forbidden plant in the mountains—Netherthorn, a poison only spoken of in myths. I offered it—cloaked in flattery—to one of the strongest Protectors. As he grew weak, I drained him of his powers, and with them, I unlocked my first element: Water.

After that, I hunted others in secret. One by one, I stole their elemental cores—Shadow from a hidden assassin, and Dark from the spirit of a cursed cave. But when the truth emerged... they cast me out. I was rusticated. Banished. Broken.

And so I swore—one day, I would take back Mesophia. Not as a student, not as a protector... but as its conqueror."

A long silence followed. Then Drake stood, his cloak of shadow billowing with unnatural wind.

"My childhood was stolen. Their lands, herbs, protectors—everything—will become mine. Their present will suffer as I did in the past."

Suddenly, a thunderous explosion shattered the stillness. A burst of red fire flared from the nearby forest.

"What was that?!" exclaimed Bot-20.

Drake smiled darkly. "That, my dear Bot-20, is the end of Mesophia. Behold—my latest creation: the Cluster Bombs. Each unit is infused with sentient fire, capable of launching destructive fireballs over miles. They sense, track, and eliminate targets with terrifying precision. They are faster, stronger, and crueler than anything Mesophia has ever faced."

Bot-20's eyes widened. "That will be our ultimate weapon!"

Drake nodded. "Yes. But it is only one of many. I also have an arsenal of corrupt machines, and now... this." He pulled a small, jagged device from his cloak. It pulsed with eerie violet light. "This gadget can twist any heart, corrupt any soul. It will make allies into enemies. Light into darkness."

He turned toward a large iron door. "Let's test it... on Alinbell."

They entered the dimly lit prison chamber. Alinbell, once bright-eyed and fierce, now sat weakly behind enchanted bars.

"Hmm... Drake?" she croaked, startled. "Why are you here?"

Drake smirked. "To test my newest invention, dear Alinbell. It's going to be fun."

"No matter what you do... someone will stop you," she whispered.

He pointed the device at her and fired.

A pulse of dark energy wrapped around her body. Her eyes turned from sapphire to blood red. Her aura blackened. Her voice became cold.

"Master," she said, kneeling before

him. "Give me your orders."

Bot-20 gasped. "It worked?!"

Drake chuckled. "Indeed. She is now... one of us. An evil protector of the dark empire."

But high above, hidden in the shadows of the rafters, a cloaked figure watched.

"A plan this evil cannot be ignored," the stranger whispered calmly. "I must find the Wheezer—Clamp—and warn the people of Mesophia. The war has begun."

The figure vanished into the night, heading toward Mesophia with haste.

5. The Junior Wizard Walter

Clamp and Nimbus were having a good day when suddenly they saw a boy that was coming running to him from a distance.

It seemed like that Clamp seemed to be in a big hurry to meet them. As the person came near to the two fellow friends, the two came to him and spoke that why are you in a hurry to meet us mister, we are just ordinary boys of the town.

"Well, the name is Walter and I am a junior student of the Beauxbacon

Academy of Magic, Mesophia. I want to inform you both that Drake, the evil wizard of Mesophia will be coming for the attack in Mesophia. I was hiding in the palace of Drake because Alinbell told me to do so and inform you about the war. And I have a very bad news for you two, I have seen Drake making new inventions and testing it on Alinbell, she grew mad, her eyes gleamed blood red. He continued We should make a team for the betterment of Mesophia. Clamp and Nimbus were shocked to hear the news. Walter's words filled them with a sense of urgency and purpose. They knew that they had to act fast. "Walter, thank you for coming to us with this information. We will do everything in our power to protect Mesophia," said Clamp, determination shining in his eyes. Nimbus nodded in agreement. "We will gather all the help we can get. We need to form a strong team to stand against Drake and his evil plans." As the sun dipped below the horizon, casting a warm, amber glow across the rolling hills of Mesophia, Clamp and Nimbus, two courageous adventurers, stood side by side on the highest peak in the land. They had come here to gaze upon the beauty of their homeland and to discuss the grave news they had received: the evil sorcerer Drake had returned from the dead, seeking vengeance against the land and its people. With a sense of determination and duty weighing heavily on their hearts, they knew that they must act swiftly to gather allies and prepare for the impending battle.

"Clamp wake up, you lazy boy" Said Clamp's mom in a angry voice "your friends are waiting for you downstairs. I think they want to meet you".

"Very well, ok just cool down for a minute it's only 7 in the morning' I am going ok?!" replied Clamp.

Later Clamp invited his friends upstairs, all had lovely breakfast and went down to talk and find more about what to do and where to go for the teams.

"So where to go next? Walter, to of course find our team members to protect Mesophia and its people" said Clamp excitedly. "Well, well, I think someone's in a hurry, well you should wait for a moment my friends, as the upcoming days of your lives are very precious, and full of danger and adventure." Replied Walter wisely "You should pack up your backpacks keeping in mind that we will not return until 2 or 3 months. We will gather a strong team that will protect Mesophia forever"

6. YorkLand Woods, Here We Come!

The time had finally come. Clamp, Walter, and Nimbus were no longer just protectors—they were now the chosen ones. They were to leave the sacred lands of Mesophia in search of allies, warriors, and ancient powers that could turn the tide against Drake's rising darkness.

But before destiny could take them across the skies, there was one last scene unfolding at Clamp's house.

"Thanks, Mom, but I don't need all this equipment," Clamp said as he fastened his gloves. "I'm going on a real mission this time—a trail that could decide the fate of Mesophia."

His mother looked up from the pouch she was preparing, her eyes firm yet filled with love. "And I'm telling you, Clamp you WILL take these". The wilds beyond Mesophia are filled with predators and pests that carry disease and darkness alike. You may have your elements... but even warriors fall to fevers."

Clamp sighed, then took the bundle. "Alright, alright... I'll keep them. But only because you won't let me leave otherwise."

A honk sounded outside the house.

"CLAMP! Come on already!" came

Walter's voice from the front. "We're not waiting all day!"

Nimbus peeked around him with a raised eyebrow. "Are we really going to leave without him, Walter?"

Walter smirked. "Of course not. I'm just trying to hurry him up."

Clamp swung his bag over his shoulder and burst through the door. "I'm here now! Ready when you are. Jet-mobile is fuelled!"

Walter raised a hand. "Hold up. We're not taking your flashy speedster today. Not where we're headed."

Clamp blinked. "We're not?"

"Nope," said Nimbus, stepping forward. "Our first destination is YorkLand Woods home to the most powerful archers in the entire cosmos. The only way there is by air. And not just any air the Skyblaze."

Clamp's mouth fell open. "The Skyblazed airplane?! That old relic still flies?"

Walter grinned. "With luck and a little magic, yes. And lucky for us, it's still docked at the Mesophian Airport—for another twenty minutes."

The trio raced across the stone-paved roads toward Mesophian Airport, their boots echoing through the dawn-washed streets. As they reached the terminal, the Skyblaze stood waiting—its silver wings gleaming under the rising sun, glowing faintly with enchanted energy. They barely made it before the doors sealed shut behind them.

As the plane took off, the friends stared through the crystalline windows, watching the lands of Mesophia disappear beneath a sea of clouds. Towering mountains loomed in the distance, their snowcaps reflecting golden sunlight. But amidst the breathtaking beauty... something dark stirred.

Clamp's eyes narrowed. "There. Look—on that cliffside."

In the shadow of a broken boulder, a black mist oozed into the soil like ink through water. Birds lay lifeless. Vines shriveled on contact.

"That's... Drake's energy," Clamp

muttered. "It's spreading."

Walter's jaw clenched. "Then we need to move fast. YorkLand Woods may be beautiful—but we're not there for sightseeing. We need allies. Now."

Nimbus nodded, though his stomach rumbled. "I agree... but also, I'm starving."

Clamp chuckled. "You're right. I could eat a forest bear right now."

He flipped open the in-seat menu. "Let's see... I'll order some blossom leaves, three bottles of costen-coke, a cheesy soy burger, and a seasoned chili pizza."

"Whoa, Clamp," said Walter, laughing. "Feeding an army?"

"Just fuelling one," Clamp replied,

smiling.

The plane roared above the clouds, pushing forward toward a new chapter. "YorkLand Woods, here we come."

7. Yorkland Woods, Lands of Archers

When the Skyblaze finally touched down on the mossy landing strip nestled within a clearing, the door opened to reveal a realm untouched by war.

The trio stepped out into YorkLand Woods—and were immediately enveloped in an atmosphere of magic and ancient beauty.

The air was crisp and earthy. Sunbeams filtered through an emerald canopy so thick that it turned sunlight into rainbows. Birds with feathers like gems sang overhead. The trees stood like ancient towers twisting, sprawling, timeless.

"Surely, friends," whispered Nimbus, eyes wide with wonder, "this place is heaven. I could live here forever."

Clamp scanned the treetops with a practiced gaze. "Don't get too comfortable. A place these peaceful hides its dangers well. I'm sure they've laid traps for outsiders."

Walter nodded. "Especially outsiders headed to recruit their greatest warrior."

They walked cautiously through the woods, navigating tight clearings, climbing vine bridges, and descending into narrow forest trails. Then, beyond a curtain of silver mist—they found it.

A village unlike any other.

The hidden settlement of Lunarian was alive literally. Its huts were shaped like tree hollows, its streets made of woven vines. Buildings curved upward like blooming flowers, and bridges fluttered with glistening wings of bark and silk. Gliding gracefully through the air were the villagers women with flowing hair, luminous wings, and eyes that shimmered with moonlight. Their clothing was spun from leaf-thread and starlight.

A wise figure approached the village elder.

She had the gentle face of a doe and a body part bark, part bloom. Her voice carried with it the rhythm of centuries.

"You are not of the forest," she said. "But you carry purpose. Come. Speak your cause."

Inside her hut—crafted into the trunk of a living oak—the air was dense with knowledge. Scrolls, relics, and celestial maps lined the walls.

"We seek warriors," Walter began. "And power not for glory, but to stop Drake."

At the name, the elder's brow darkened.

"You are brave to speak his name here. Yes... we know of him. And yes, Princess Olivia of YorkLand is our greatest archer. But you will need more than arrows to stop him. You need the forest itself." She stood.

"There is a place deep within the trees. A sacred grove home to the Forest Lord, a being of old power and spirit. If he deems your hearts worthy, he may bless you with the strength you seek."

The journey was not easy.

They crossed rivers roaring with enchanted currents, scaled giant roots taller than towers, and passed whispering groves where trees seemed to move. But finally, from the peak of a lookout tree, the elder pointed ahead.

"There," she said, voice soft as wind, "that is the Sacred Grove."

In its centre stood a titanic oak, older than time itself. As they approached, the air grew heavier—as if magic pressed against their chests.

The elder bowed. "Oh, Forest Lord... hear our call."

The tree creaked... then split.

From within the bark emerged a massive stag, antlers adorned with ivy and crystals, his eyes glowing amber-red like fire caught in honey. His voice rumbled across the ground like thunder through roots.

"I sense your desire. I see your courage," the stag said. "But power is not given freely. You must earn the Forest's trust. If you fail, the Grove will reject you forever."

Clamp stepped forward. "We accept the trials."

Walter and Nimbus stood beside him. "Together."

The Forest Lord's eyes narrowed. "Then prepare yourselves. Your hearts, your minds, and your souls... will all be tested."

And so, their greatest trial began—not of strength, but of spirit.

8. The Trial Begins

The majestic stag turned solemnly to the elder, who gave a respectful nod.

"The first trial," she said, her voice calm but commanding, "is one of strength and endurance. You must follow the path of the rising sun, through the untamed forest. Along the way, you will face challenges designed to test your body, your will, and your heart. Should you succeed, you will be blessed with the strength of the Forest Beasts."

Without another word, the stag melted back into the bark of the great oak. The elder motioned for the group to follow her into the dense forest. Faded, moss-covered markings on the trees guided their path, but the underbrush was thick, and the terrain unforgiving.

The journey was gruelling. Their legs burned, lungs ached, and sweat poured down their faces. They ran tirelessly, leaping over twisted roots and ducking under low-hanging vines. A chilling howl echoed in the distance.

Soon they arrived at a wide river cutting across the forest. A pack of wolves—massive, silver-furred, and growling—stood guard on the bank. The elder stepped forward and spoke to them in the tongue of beasts, her words melodic and ancient. After a tense pause, the wolves bowed their heads and stepped aside, honouring the forest's blessing.

The journey continued—across rivers, under cascading waterfalls, and through thick fog. Illusions whispered in the dark, phantom shadows moving in the corners of their vision, branches snapping behind them. The elder reminded them to stay focused.

Finally, they stumbled into a moonlit clearing. The great stag waited. Its antlers shimmered with ethereal light.

"You have proven yourselves thus far," the stag intoned, its deep voice echoing through the glade. "Now comes the trial of wisdom. You must journey to the World Tree. There lies a relic of immense power, locked within a chest guarded by an ancient beast. Only those pure of heart may unlock it. Use your minds. Use your unity. If your hearts remain true, the relic shall be yours."

The elder pointed west, toward the setting sun. "Follow its path. But beware—the guardian beast does not yield easily. And the forest will watch."

They moved deeper into the forest, where daylight faded into a golden dusk. The trees grew older here—wiser. Their branches twisted like ancient fingers, whispering secrets in the wind.

At last, they reached it.

The World Tree.

It stood in silence at the centre of a vast clearing, its colossal trunk spiralling toward the heavens, branches wide enough to cradle clouds. The very air around it shimmered with power.

In front of the tree stood the guardian beast—an enormous hybrid of lion and serpent. Its mane burned like embers, and its long-scaled tail coiled in the grass, flicking with tension. Its eyes locked onto the group, glowing with ancient intellect.

The elder stepped forward and began chanting in a haunting, melodic language none of them understood. Her voice washed over the creature like a lullaby. After a long moment, the beast's posture softened. It lowered its head and moved aside.

Behind it sat an ornately carved chest. The wood gleamed with unnatural light. At its centre was a large ruby, pulsing with life.

"This is the final test," the elder said. "To open it, you must solve its riddle. The answer lies in the objects you carry—each chosen by instinct, not by accident."

They reached into their packs.

Walter pulled out a polished stone, Nimbus a delicate feather, Clamp a hand-carved wooden toy, and from Nimbus's bag tumbled a strand of bright yarn. They stared at each other, unsure.

"The riddle is inscribed upon the

chest," whispered the elder. "Take the stone, the feather, the string, and the toy, and place them as they are—but with a twist. The combination lies within their names—rearranged, not replaced!"

Walter laid the stone first. "This is the trunk—the strength—the core."

Nimbus carefully tied the string around the stone. "The string connects us all. It binds past, present, and future."

Clamp placed the toy atop the knotted bundle. "This is joy. Youth. The future. And perhaps... the answer."

Nimbus then gently placed the feather over it all. "And this," he whispered, "is the freedom that carries us forward."

As they arranged the items, the ruby on the chest began to glow brighter—pulsing, breathing. Then, with a click, the lid opened.

Inside was a single scroll, wrapped in golden threads, and sealed with the emblem of the Forest Lord.

The stag appeared once more, stepping from the shadows.

"You have passed the trials of body and mind," it said. "Your courage and unity are unquestionable. You shall be granted the mark of Polis—the Ancient Archer Beast of the Woodlands. His spirit shall guide your aim and shield your souls in the battles to come."

The scroll rose from the chest, glowing, before splitting into three beams of light—each striking Clamp, Walter, and Nimbus in the chest. Their bodies shimmered briefly as the power of the forest settled within them.

"Go now," said the elder. "You have been chosen. But remember, this power is not for glory—it is for protection, for love, and for balance. Use it well, warriors of Mesophia."

As the forest whispered around them, and the World Tree hummed with approval, the heroes knew their journey had truly begun.

They began their quest on recurring the great warrior of Yorkland!

9. Princess Olivia and Her Test

Their quest led them to the hidden palace of Princess Olivia, the greatest archer to ever live. Clamp, Nimbus, and Walter had heard tales of her prowess with a bow and arrow, and they knew that with her by their side, they stood a chance against the evil Drake. As they approached the palace gates, they were greeted by a lone guard standing at attention. His armor was polished to a mirror-like shine, and his sword was held firmly in his hand. He eyed the three friends warily, clearly suspicious of their motives.

Clamp stepped forward, his posture straight and his voice steady. “We come in peace, my respectable sir. We seek an audience with Princess Olivia.”

The guard’s expression softened slightly. “Indeed? And what business could you three have with the princess?”

Clamp cleared his throat. “We come seeking her aid, my good man. Our home, Mesophia, is in grave danger. An evil being called Drake threatens to destroy everything we hold dear.”

The guard’s eyes widened in surprise. “Truly? I had not heard of such a threat.”

“Yes,” said Clamp gravely. “We have come seeking allies to help us protect Mesophia, and we believe that Princess

Olivia's skills with a bow and arrow would be invaluable in our fight against Drake."

The guard considered their words for a moment, then nodded slowly. "Very well," he said. "I will inform the princess of your presence. Please wait here." With that, he turned on his heel and disappeared into the palace, leaving the three friends to wait nervously outside.

As they waited, Clamp, Nimbus, and Walter exchanged anxious glances. The sun dipped below the horizon, bathing the sky in hues of red and orange. Stars began to twinkle in the velvety blackness above. They were grateful for the distraction, for it took their minds off the impending audience with

Princess Olivia. After what seemed like an eternity, the palace gates swung open once more. The guard emerged, his expression solemn. “The princess will see you now,” he said, gesturing for them to follow.

Clamp, Nimbus, and Walter exchanged nervous glances before following the guard into the palace. The halls were ornate beyond measure, with rich tapestries adorning the walls and golden chandeliers hanging from high ceilings. The three friends felt small and insignificant as they were led through the grand hallways, their footsteps muffled by the plush red carpet.

After what seemed like an eternity

of walking, they were finally ushered into Princess Olivia's throne room. The room was dominated by a massive throne of polished black marble, upon which sat the princess herself. She was a strikingly beautiful, her long, raven hair, and her piercing green eyes fixed upon them. Her bow and quiver of arrows were slung over her shoulder, and her armor was adorned with the insignia of the great archers' guild.

Clamp, Nimbus, and Walter bowed deeply before her, their hearts pounding with a mix of fear and determination. Princess Olivia studied them for a long moment before speaking. "So, you three have come seeking my aid against this Drake?"

Clamp straightened, his shoulders squared. "Yes, your Highness. Our home, Mesophia, is in grave danger. Drake threatens to destroy everything we hold. We have come seeking allies to help us fight against him, and we believe that with your skills as our leader, we stand a chance of prevailing."

Princess Olivia leaned back in her throne, considering their words. "I see. And what makes you think that I would risk my life and reputation to aid you in your fight?"

Clamp took a deep breath before answering. "Because, your Highness, the danger that Drake poses is not only to Mesophia, but to all of Yorkland. If he were to defeat us, he would continue his rampage unchecked, destroying everything in his path. We believe that we should make an alliance and then only we will have the strength to defeat him, and that together, we can defeat him!"

Nimbus stepped forward, his voice steady and determined. "We also believe, Princess Olivia, that there is more at stake here than just our homes and our lives. This is a battle between good and evil, and we are asking you to join us in the fight for what is right. We will be eternally grateful for your aid, and we will do whatever it takes to ensure that your sacrifice is not in vain."

The princess regarded them silently for a moment, her expression thoughtful. Finally, she spoke. “Very well,” she said. “I will help you, but on one condition. If you can win me in a contest of skill, I will join you in your fight against Drake.”

Clamp, Nimbus, and Walter exchanged glances, their hearts leaping with hope. “Your Highness, we would be honored to compete against you in any contest you should choose,” Clamp said, his voice steady. “What do you have in mind?”

The princess smiled. “Very well. I propose a contest of archery. You three will compete against me, one on one. If you manage to defeat me, I will pledge my allegiance to your cause and join you in the fight against Drake."

Clamp, Nimbus, and Walter nodded eagerly. "We accept your challenge, Princess Olivia. We are confident in our abilities, and we will do whatever it takes to defeat you."

The princess smiled grimly. "Then let the contest begin."

She rose from her throne and led them to a grand hallway at the far end of the throne room. At the end of the hall was a large, open field, with targets set up at various distances. The targets were painted with the colors of the four elements: red for fire, blue for water, green for earth, and white for air.

10. The Competition Begins!

As they approached the field, Princess Olivia removed her bow and arrow from her quiver, expertly stringing the bow with a single fluid motion. She turned to the three friends, her eyes glinting with challenge. “You three will each take turns shooting at the targets,” she said, her voice steady and commanding. “For each target you hit, you will earn one point. The one who will bring the Fire target down, will face me in the final round.”

Clamp, Nimbus, and Walter nodded

in understanding. As they took their places at the starting line, Princess Olivia raised her hand, signaling for them to begin.

The first of the three friends to compete was Nimbus. He took a deep breath, focusing his energy on the target before him. With a fluid motion, he released his arrow, aiming for the blue target representing water. The arrow flew through the air, hitting the center of the target with a satisfying thud. The crowd let out a murmur of approval.

Next up was Clamp. He narrowed his eyes, concentrating on the task at hand. He knocked an arrow, took aim, and released it in one smooth motion. His arrow soared through the air, striking the green target with unerring accuracy. Another murmur rippled through the crowd as they acknowledged his skill.

As Walter stepped up to the line, he took a deep breath, trying to calm his nerves. With a steady hand, he took aim at the fire target and released his arrow. It flew gracefully through the air, hitting the center of the target with deadly precision.

The crowd erupted into cheers as Walter turned to face the princess, his chest swelling with pride. She nodded at him respectfully, acknowledging his skill. The final round was about to begin, and the fate of the world hung in the balance.

Walter was nervous yet excited. As he took aim at his target, Olivia could see the determination in his stance. She knew that she would have to be at her best to defeat him. Olivia also marked her arrow and pointed at the target.

The air was still and quiet as the two of them waited for the other to make a move. Time seemed to slow down as they held their breath, the tension palpable. Finally, Walter released his arrow, and it flew through the air, heading straight for the center of the target. The princess watched it with narrowed eyes, her heart racing. She knew that she could not afford to make even the slightest mistake.

With practiced ease, she drew back

her bow, aiming at the same target that Walter had chosen. Her arrow left the bow with a whistling sound, cutting through the air with deadly precision. It collided with Walter's arrow mid-flight, sending both arrows spinning out of control. The crowd gasped in surprise as the arrows fell harmlessly to the ground.

Walter's jaw dropped in disbelief. He had never seen anyone in his wizarding life move that fast, let alone match his skill with a bow and arrow. Princess Olivia stepped forward, her chest heaving from the exertion. She looked at him with respect and admiration. "You are indeed a worthy opponent," she said, her voice steady. "But I am still the victor."

The crowd erupted into cheers and applause, hailing Princess Olivia as the champion. She bowed graciously, acknowledging their praise. But as she turned to Clamp, Nimbus, and Walter, her expression turned serious. "Your skills are unparalleled," she said. "You three have proven yourselves to be a fine archer in the land. She motioned to join them at the front of the field. As they approached, she continued, "I have seen the way you work together, the trust you have in one another. It is this bond that I believe will help us save the world."

With this saying they all with Princess Olivia will be returning to

Mesophia the next day.

Our heroes have managed to find one ally for the protection of mesophia but will they be able to find more of them because they will surely need more than that to defeat Drake and his Team.

11. Soroshia of Mesophia

"Mesophia, a land of vibrant colors and aromas, was nestled between the arid desert to the west and the lush tropics to the east. Its people, known as Mesophians, were a resilient and adaptable bunch, having learned to survive in the harsh yet breathtakingly beautiful environment that surrounded them. Their culture was a unique blend of traditional customs and modern innovations, reflected in everything from their intricate architecture to their exquisite cuisine. Princess

Olivia, the young and curious ruler of the realm, was about to embark on a journey through the heart of Mesophia, accompanied by her friends: Clamp, Nimbus, and Walter. As they made their way through the dense jungle, winding their way towards the fabled train station, they couldn't help but share stories about their homeland with their eager audience."

One of the most fascinating aspects of Mesophian culture, as Clamp explained, was their unique system of government. Rather than relying on a single monarch, Mesophia was governed by a council of elders, who had been chosen by their communities for their wisdom, experience, and selflessness. This system ensured that decisions were made with the best interests of the people at heart, and that no one individual had too much power. The princess found this concept particularly intriguing, as it was quite different from the traditional monarchical system she was used to.

As they continued their journey, they encountered a variety of flora and fauna native to Mesophia. Nimbus, who was an expert botanist, pointed out various plants with medicinal properties, explaining how Mesophians used them to treat common ailments. They also came across a small herd of creatures known as "pufflings," which were adorable, furry animals that resembled a cross between a rabbit and a squirrel. Walter, who had a particular fondness for animals, was delighted to see them and spent some time watching the friendly creatures.

The sight was breathtaking: hundreds of fields stretching out as far as the eye could see, each one a patchwork of vibrant greens and blues. Clamp explained that rice was not only a staple food in Mesophia, but it was also central to their culture and traditions. Rice was used to make delicious dishes, as well as being an important part of their celebrations and ceremonies. As they neared the train station, they could hear the familiar whistle in the distance. Excitement filled the air as they finally caught sight of the train, its gleaming carriages adorned with intricate designs and vibrant colors. The doors of the train slid open, revealing a lavishly decorated interior filled with comfortable seating and elegant furnishings. A friendly Mesophian conductor greeted them with a warm smile and offered them a seat in their private room. Once settled in, Princess Olivia couldn't help but marvel at the luxurious surroundings. The walls were adorned with beautiful paintings depicting scenes from Mesophian history and folklore, while soft music played over the speakers, filling the air with a soothing ambiance. A servant appeared with a tray of refreshments, offering them a selection of delicacies native to Mesophia: sweet pastries packed with exotic fruits, fragrant drinks, and cool Cocoa flavored water.

As the train chugged along, Walter regaled the group with tales of the grand festivals and celebrations that took place in Mesophia. He described how entire villages would come together to celebrate the harvest, dancing and singing throughout the night beneath a canopy of stars. Nimbus added that these gatherings were also an opportunity for Mesophians to share their knowledge and skills with one another, ensuring that their unique culture would continue to thrive for generations to come.

Clamp, who had been quietly observing the scenery outside the window, pointed out several structures along the tracks that were unlike anything Olivia had seen before. "Those are our aqueducts," he explained. "They were built hundreds of years ago to bring fresh water from the mountains to the rice paddies and our villages." The princess was amazed at the ingenuity and perseverance of the Mesophian people, who had managed to create such an intricate system to support their communities.

12. Nexus City of Dreams

Eventually, the train arrived at their final destination: a bustling city named Nexus. The city was unlike anything Olivia had ever seen before; it was a cosmopolitan metropolis with tall buildings, wide boulevards, and a vibrant energy that was infectious. As they disembarked from the train, they were greeted by a group of young Mesophian children who were excited to show them around their city.

Over the next few days, they explored Nexus, visiting its famous museums, art galleries, and historic landmarks. They also sampled the city's delicious cuisine, which combined elements from both traditional Mesophian cooking and foreign influences. One evening, they attended a concert at the city's outdoor amphitheater, where they listened to a mesmerizing performance by a local orchestra. The music was unlike anything Princess Olivia had ever heard before, with its unique blend of Western melodies and harmonies. There was a museum of medicines. It also had many ancient herbs that were guarded by thousands of Guards who were specially trained to do so. The city of Nexus, nestled amidst rolling hills and verdant valleys, was once a haven of peace and prosperity. However, recent events have cast a sinister shadow over the landscape. A series of brazen robberies have plagued the city, each more daring than the last. The most infamous of these heists involved the theft of the precious gem of St. Stanely, a relic that had been safeguarded by the city's finest for centuries. The mastermind behind this audacious caper was none other than James, a ruthless and cunning robber whose name struck fear into the hearts of all who dared to cross his path.

The news of the theft dominated the airwaves, with news anchors frantically reporting on the whereabouts of James and the precious gem. As the friends gathered, the group discussed their plan of action. Clamp would lead the charge, using his brute strength and unyielding courage to confront James head-on. Nimbus, ever the cunning strategist, would remain behind the scenes, using his arcane powers to manipulate the environment and turn the tide of battle in their favor. Walter, the Junior Wizard would provide cover and take down any of James's cohorts who dared to stand in their way. Finally, Princess Olivia, though young and great archer, would prove to be an invaluable asset with her keen eyesight and unwavering determination.

As they prepared for the showdown, the group couldn't help but feel a sense of trepidation. They knew that they were up against one of the most dangerous criminals in the land. With a renewed sense of purpose, they set out into the night, ready to face whatever challenges lay ahead, whether they are from the city or from somebody else.

13. The Heistbreaker's Reckoning

The city of Nexus shimmered beneath a sky of stars, but Clamp and his companions had no time to admire its beauty. With the theft of the Gem of St. Stanely still sending shockwaves across Mesophia, they had a mission—to find and stop James before he vanished into legend.

The group gathered in a quiet warehouse near the city's outer ring, poring over maps and clues. Nimbus traced a finger over an alley near the old Nexus aqueducts. "This is where the last sighting happened. James never runs without a backdoor—he's hiding somewhere with an escape route."

Clamp cracked his knuckles. "Then let's make sure he doesn't get to use it."

Night cloaked their movements as they approached the abandoned foundry. Rusted pipes hissed, and shadows shifted unnaturally. Walter muttered a spell under his breath, and glowing glyphs floated around them like protective fireflies.

Suddenly, a blade flashed.

A trap had been sprung.

James's men—agile, masked, and trained—sprang from the rooftops. But the heroes were ready. Clamp charged forward like a battering ram, scattering attackers with brute force. Walter summoned a shimmering barrier to protect Olivia as arrows flew past them, and Nimbus sent arcs of lightning racing along the iron beams overhead, shorting out the enemy's enchanted tools.

James emerged from the smoke like a phantom, his black cloak swirling, the Gem of St. Stanely gleaming at his chest. "Ah, I hate pests, especially the one who come in my way!"

"You've stolen more than a gem," Clamp replied, "You've stolen peace. And we're here to take it back."

With unnatural speed, James lunged, his twin daggers spinning. Clamp ducked and fired. Olivia intercepted him, Arrows against steel, but James was like smoke—hard to hit, harder to hold.

Nimbus, keeping his distance, whispered an incantation and pointed to the ground. Vines erupted from the cracks, grabbing at James's legs. He twisted midair and sliced through them—but just enough time had been bought.

Walter shouted, "NOW!"

Olivia drew a silver-tipped arrow, its shaft glowing with blue runes. She released it, and it hit James square in the gem.

A burst of light exploded.

James screamed, stumbling as the gem cracked and flared wildly. "You...